OTHER YEARLING BOOKS
BY PATRICIA REILLY G

THE KIDS OF THE P

THE BEAST IN MS

FISH

THE CANDY C

DECEMBER SECRETS

IN THE DINOSAUR'S PAW

BEAST AND THE HALLOWEEN HORROR

EMILY ARROW PROMISES TO DO BETTER THIS YEAR

MONSTER RABBIT RUNS AMUCK!

WAKE UP, EMILY, IT'S MOTHER'S DAY!

Plus the Polk Street Specials:

WRITE UP A STORM WITH THE POLK STREET SCHOOL

COUNT YOUR MONEY WITH THE POLK STREET SCHOOL

THE POSTCARD PEST

TURKEY TROUBLE

THE LINCOLN LIONS BAND

MEET THE LINCOLN LIONS BAND

YANKEE DOODLE DRUMSTICKS

THE "JINGLE BELLS" JAM

ROOTIN' TOOTIN' BUGLE BOY

THE RED, WHITE, AND BLUE VALENTINE

THE GREAT SHAMROCK DISASTER

YEARLING BOOKS / YOUNG YEARLINGS / YEARLING CLASSICS are designed especially to entertain and enlighten young people. Patricia Reilly Giff, consultant to this series, received her bachelor's degree from Marymount College and a master's degree in history from St. John's University. She holds a Professional Diploma in Reading and a Doctorate of Humane Letters from Hofstra University. She was a teacher and reading consultant for many years, and is the author of numerous books for young readers.

For a complete listing of all Yearling titles, write to
Dell Readers Service, P.O. Box 1045,
South Holland, IL 60473.

Show Time at the Polk Street School

Published by
Bantam Doubleday Dell Books for Young Readers
a division of
Bantam Doubleday Dell Publishing Group, Inc.
1540 Broadway
New York, New York 10036

ISBN: 0-440-40962-4

Reprinted by arrangement with Delacorte Press
Printed in the United States of America

February 1995

10 9 8 7 6 5 4 3 2 1

SHOW TIME AT THE POLK STREET SCHOOL:

PLAYS YOU CAN DO YOURSELF OR IN THE CLASSROOM

Patricia Reilly Giff

Illustrated by Blanche Sims

A YEARLING BOOK

To Carol Geller,
who loved plays and the world of the theater . . .
whose inspiration, suggestions,
and painstaking work helped to
make this book what it is.

I look up and see you walking.

• CONTENTS •

Talking About . . . Plays 1

Acting . . . *The Candy Corn Contest* 5

Thinking About . . . a Mystery 37

Acting . . . *The Secret at the Polk Street School* 39

Trying Out . . . Different Ideas 73

Acting . . . *Fancy Feet* 75

Talking about . . . Plays

"It's play time," says Ms. Rooney.

Beast sits up straight. "Great!" he says. "I love to play."

"Not *that* kind of play," says Dawn Bosco. "It's the stage kind, with parts, and props, and an audience."

"Right," says Ms. Rooney. "Let's talk about it."

Emily Arrow waves her hand in the air. "I know something. When you get your part, try to be just like the person you're playing. Close your eyes for a minute.

Make believe you're right inside that person's skin."

"I hope I don't get the part of a skunk," says Matthew.

"Or a snake," Beast says.

Dawn Bosco raises her hand. "I know something to tell Beast." She looks around at him. "Don't wiggle around all over the stage—"

Sherri Dent cuts in. "And don't wave to your friends in the audience . . ."

"I always forget my part." Beast sounds worried.

"He's probably going to ruin the whole thing," says Sherri Dent.

"Probably," says Dawn Bosco.

"No," says Emily. "If you forget your part, make it up as you go along."

"If we have too many lines to remember," Ms. Rooney says, "we'll write them out on paper. We can read them to the audience."

Beast taps Matthew's arm. "Too bad we don't know how to read."

"One last thing," Dawn Bosco says. "If your costume starts to fall off, don't pay any attention. Just keep going."

"You've got the idea," says Ms. Rooney. "We'll start with *The Candy Corn Contest*."

Acting . . .
THE CANDY CORN CONTEST

• *CHARACTERS (The people in the play):*

MS. ROONEY

The class: ALEX, BEAST, DAWN, DERRICK, EMILY, HOLLY, JASON, JILL, MATTHEW, NOAH, SHERRI, TIMOTHY, WAYNE

• *SETTING (What the stage looks like):*

Ms. Rooney's classroom with desks, a chalkboard, and a wall clock.

• *PROPERTIES (Things you'll need):*

Brown chalk
Lunch bag with a sandwich
Jar filled with candy corn
Cookbook
Library book
Schoolbooks for each student
Sweater

Apples
Box of raisins
Wad of string
Small pencil
Crumpled piece of paper
Loose candy corn (several pieces)
Bowl
Large pot to make applesauce

• *COSTUMES:*

Children in Ms. Rooney's class will wear everyday clothes. It's almost Thanksgiving. If you live in a place that's not too warm, some children might wear sweaters.

Ms. Rooney might wear a skirt and blouse. Tie a scarf around the blouse collar or around her shoulders. You might want to add a dark-blue button-down sweater.

• *MAKEUP:*

For Ms. Rooney's hair: If your hair is long, you can wear it up in a bun. If your hair is medium length or short, don't wear barrettes or ribbons.

Remember Ms. Rooney likes orange lip gloss. She likes earrings, too.

Use a little eye shadow and some blush. Make her look elegant!

The class should use makeup, too. The

coloring of our faces fades under bright lights onstage. Makeup helps the audience see us better. So darken eyebrows; put blush on your cheeks. The girls might wear lipstick.

• SCENE 1 •

MS. ROONEY *is standing at the chalkboard. She traces her hand with brown chalk.*

MS. R: Today we're going to talk about Thanksgiving. This is the way to draw a Thanksgiving turkey.

[BEAST *puts his hand into his desk. He starts to open his lunch bag. The bag crackles. (It crackles a lot.)* MATTHEW *turns around, and they begin to laugh.*]

MS. R: I have some exciting news.

[*She holds up a jar filled with candy corn.*]

We're going to have a contest. Guess how many pieces of candy are in this jar?

EMILY: Two hundred thousand.

DAWN: That's not right. Maybe a hundred.

NOAH: What's the prize?

MS. R: The whole jar of candy corn. It will be a Thanksgiving present from me.
[MATTHEW *gives* BEAST *a poke.*]

MATTHEW: I hope I win. If you win, will you go halves with me?
[BEAST *looks out the window. He makes believe he hasn't heard* MATTHEW.]

EMILY: How many guesses do we get?

MS. R: That's the fun part. Every time

you read a page of your library book, you can take a guess.

MATTHEW: Ohhhh, noooo. I'm a terrible reader.

TIMOTHY: Great!

[BEAST *whispers to* MATTHEW.]

BEAST: Timothy is the fastest reader in the class. He'll probably win. Too bad.

EMILY: I'm going to try to win.

MS. R: Good for you.

BEAST: Emily's a terrible reader, just like us.

[BEAST *pulls his library book out from his desk.*]

This book is too fat and hard.

I'm going to get a nice skinny one.

MS. R: No cheating. No reading skinny little baby books.
[BEAST *taps* MATTHEW'*s arm.*]

BEAST: If I win, I'll share with you.

MS. R: Can anyone tell us about the first Thanksgiving?

TIMOTHY: I can.

DAWN: Me, too.

MS. R: Many years ago some people sailed across the ocean.
[EMILY *raises her hand.*]

EMILY: They came on a boat called the *Mayflower.*

MS. R: Right, Emily. The people were called Pilgrims. It was cold. The Pilgrims had very little food. Many of them were sick. The Pilgrims' first winter was terrible.

[NOAH *raises his hand.*]

NOAH: Then the Indians came to help them.

MS. R: Very good, Noah. Are you listening, Beast?

[BEAST *is hiding behind* MATTHEW. *He is eating his lunch. He jumps.*]

BEAST: Yes.

ALEX: The Indians showed the Pilgrims how to plant corn. They told them to put dead fish in the earth with the seed. It would make the corn grow better.

JASON: Yucks.

MS. R: Don't be silly, Jason. The Indians were right. The corn grew tall and strong.
[TIMOTHY *raises his hand.*]

TIMOTHY: The Pilgrims learned to hunt, so they had more food.

MS. R: Yes. The Pilgrims worked hard. Very hard. They did the right thing.
[DAWN *raises her hand.*]

DAWN: Then they had a Thanksgiving party.

MS. R: Yes. They invited everyone.

[MS. ROONEY *looks at the clock.*] It's time to go home. For tomorrow, I want everyone to bring an apple. We'll make Thanksgiving applesauce.
[*The class packs their books. Everyone leaves but* BEAST. *He sticks his head out the door. He's looking for someone. He speaks to himself.*]

BEAST: My sister Holly always makes me wait.
[*He walks around the classroom. He picks up* MATTHEW'*s sweater from the floor. He puts it on* MATTHEW'*s chair. He walks over to* MS. ROONEY'*s desk.*]
I wonder how many pieces of candy corn there are? I'd love to eat the whole jar right now.
[*He tries to count the candy corn. He takes the top off the jar and*

pokes his finger into the jar. He takes four pieces out of the jar. He puts them on the desk. He puts three back into the jar. He pops one into his mouth. Then he reaches back into the jar and pops a second and a third piece into his mouth. He puts the top back on the jar. There's a sound at the door.]

MATTHEW: Forgot my sweater.

[BEAST *tries to talk and hide the candy corn in his mouth.*]
I wish we'd win.

BEAST: Mmm.

MATTHEW: I saw Ms. Rooney counting all the candy corn at lunchtime.

BEAST: Oh.

MATTHEW: She wrote the number on the bottom of the jar.

BEAST: I wouldn't look.

MATTHEW: I wouldn't look, either. Ms. Rooney said we're going to count them again. After someone wins. She said it will be a good math lesson.

BEAST: Oh.

MATTHEW: I'm going to work on my book tonight.

[MATTHEW *holds up his book.*]

BEAST: I can't read the name, but it looks good.

MATTHEW: I can't read the name, either. I can't even read any of the words. But it's about the rain forests. I can tell by the pictures.

BEAST: Neat.

[HOLLY *pokes her head in the classroom door.*]

HOLLY: Get moving.

BEAST: I'm coming. Stop rushing me.

[*He speaks to himself.*]
What will Ms. Rooney do when she sees that three pieces of candy corn are gone?

End of Scene 1

• SCENE 2 •

It's the next day at school. BEAST *is alone in the classroom. He is holding the candy corn jar.*

BEAST: Oh, good. No one is here. Now I can change the number on the candy corn jar. I hate to do this, but . . .
[*He looks at the number.*]
Two seventy-eight. I'll just take away three. Then I'll just forget the number.
[*There is a noise from outside. Someone is coming.* BEAST *puts the jar back on* MS. ROONEY'*s desk. He races for his seat. The class comes in.*]

MS. R: We have time for some quick candy corn guesses.

[*Several children raise their hands.* EMILY *comes to the front.* BEAST *slides down in his seat.*]

EMILY: I have two guesses. Nine hundred one.

[MS. ROONEY *shakes her head no.* EMILY *stares at the jar.*]

Six hundred sixty-eleven.

[MS. ROONEY *shakes her head.*]

DERRICK: No such number.

MS. R: Your turn, Timothy.

TIMOTHY: I have a bunch of guesses. Six hundred. Eight hundred. A thousand . . .

[MS. ROONEY *keeps shaking her head no.*]

MS. R: Too bad. We'll try again tomorrow. Right now, we're going to

make applesauce. Everyone, hold up your apples.
[*The class holds up apples.* BEAST *puts his hand up to his mouth. He's forgotten his apple.*] Beast, I don't see your apple.

BEAST: I left it home.

MATTHEW: I'll share.

MS. R: You're a good pilgrim, Matthew.

DAWN: My mother gave me a box of raisins for the applesauce.

MS. R: Another good pilgrim. I have some nice cold water in the pot. We'll take our apples and the pot down to the cafeteria.

We'll cook it there.

[*The class leaves. A few minutes later,* BEAST *and* MATTHEW *come back to the room. They look for something on* MS. ROONEY'*s desk.*]

BEAST: Ms. Rooney said it was right here.

[MATTHEW *holds up the cookbook.*]

MATTHEW: Here it is.

BEAST: I have to tell you something, Matthew.

[MATTHEW *puts the cookbook on his head. He tries to walk around with it.*]

I know how many candies there are in the jar.

MATTHEW: Really?

BEAST: Yes, I ate three. I tried to change the number on the jar. But everyone came back to class. I have to do it now.

MATTHEW: You can't do that. I think Ms. Rooney may check the fingerprints.

BEAST: Fingerprints?

MATTHEW: She'll see that the number looks different.

BEAST: No. I'll do it so you can't tell.

MATTHEW: You can't write like Ms. Rooney. She may take the jar to the police. Your fingerprints will be all over it.

BEAST: I think you're right.
[JILL *pops her head in.*]

JILL: Ms. Rooney is waiting for that cookbook.

MATTHEW: We're coming.
[JILL *leaves.*]
I have an idea.
[*He reaches into his pocket. He pulls out a bunch of things.*

String. A small pencil. A crumpled piece of paper.]

Wait a minute. I know it's here.

[*He reaches into his other pocket. He pulls out several pieces of candy corn. He opens the jar. He drops three inside. He hands one to* BEAST *and puts one in his own mouth.*]

BEAST: You saved my life, Matthew.

[*They exit the stage. A moment later, everyone returns.* MS. ROONEY *is carrying a bowl of applesauce. The class is talking.*]

NOAH: I can't wait to eat that applesauce.

WAYNE: I can't wait to see who's going to win the candy corn contest.

[BEAST *stands there, thinking. He goes to* MS. ROONEY'*s desk.*]

BEAST: I have to tell you something.

[MS. ROONEY *looks up.*]

MS. R: Go ahead, Beast.

BEAST: I ate three pieces of candy corn. Matthew gave me three more. He didn't want me to get in trouble. I thought I'd better tell you.

MS. R: A pilgrim wouldn't have eaten three pieces of candy corn.

BEAST: I know.

MS. R: But you're a true pilgrim for telling me.

[MS. ROONEY *claps her hands. Everyone takes a seat.*]
All right, class. Who has guesses?
[*Many hands are raised.*]

TIMOTHY: I have five.

EMILY: I have three.

JILL: Me, too.

BEAST: I have a guess.

MATTHEW: Me, too. I have a guess. One big one.
[*Everyone goes up to* MS. ROONEY*'s desk. After each wrong guess,* MS. ROONEY *either says no or shakes her head no.*]

JILL: Three twenty-one.

TIMOTHY: Three forty-seven. Three fifty. I'm going to think for a few minutes.

BEAST: Two hundred and . . . two hundred and . . .

[MS. ROONEY *leans forward a little. She smiles.* MATTHEW *looks at* BEAST *and shakes his head no.*]

No, three hundred. I mean . . . three forty-two.

[MS. ROONEY *leans back. She shakes her head no.*]

MS. R: Timothy?

TIMOTHY: I think it's in the two hundreds. How about two forty-one?

MS. R: No. How about Matthew?

[MATTHEW *squeezes his eyes shut.*]

MATTHEW: Two ninety-nine.

[MATTHEW *opens his eyes.* MS. ROONEY *shakes her head.*]

EMILY: My turn. I think . . . I think it's . . . two seventy-eight.

BEAST: That's it!

MS. R: You're right, Emily.

[EMILY *smiles.*]

EMILY: I don't believe it!

SHERRI: I don't believe it, either.

EMILY: Can we divide them up? Everyone can share!

[MS. ROONEY *does a dividing problem on the chalkboard. Everyone gets twenty-three pieces. There are two pieces extra.*]

Two pieces for you, Ms. Rooney.

BEAST: Terrific! There's nothing like candy corn and applesauce.

MS. R: And being good pilgrims.

[*Curtain*]

• • • • • • • • • •

Thinking About . . . a Mystery

"Plays are wonderful," says Ms. Rooney. "Some are funny. They're called *comedies.* Some are sad. They're called *tragedies.*"

Dawn Bosco reaches into her desk. She pulls out her polka dot private eye hat. "I like mysteries the best."

"Me, too," says Jason.

"Maybe we could . . ." Ms. Rooney begins.

The class claps.

Ms. Rooney holds up her hand. "Mysteries aren't easy though. You have to remember to say all the clues. If you forget and leave one out—"

"The audience can't solve the mystery," says Matthew.

Ms. Rooney nods. "Here's how to do it. Begin by reading the play. Read it several times. Be sure you know the clues. It doesn't matter if you change the words. It *does* matter that the clues remain the same."

Dawn Bosco stands up. "If you need any help, just let me know. I'm great at this."

"Let's begin," says Ms. Rooney.

Acting . . .

THE SECRET AT THE POLK STREET SCHOOL

• *CHARACTERS (The people in the play):*

MS. ROONEY

The class: ALEX, BEAST, DAWN, DERRICK, EMILY, JASON, JILL, LINDA, MATTHEW, SHERRI, TIMOTHY, and WAYNE

Others: DRAKE, LOUIE, JIM, WOLF/PEGGY, extras

• *SETTING (What the stage looks like):*

The stage is divided in half. One half is set up as a classroom. The other half is set up as an empty stage. A movable chalkboard separates the classroom from the stage. On the stage is a closet. The closet door faces away from the audience. (The closet can be a portable closet or a cardboard refrigerator or stove carton.)

Scene 2: Turn closet door toward audience for Drake's house. Put two chairs in front for Drake and Louie.

Bushes can be large plants in pots from home or the classroom. If you can't find tall plants, group as many potted plants together as you can.

- *PROPERTIES (Things you'll need):*

Books
Piece of wrinkled paper
Polka dot hat
Cake box
Can of chicken soup
Loaf of bread
Wristwatch
Cookies
Gum
Garden tools
Broom
Folded piece of paper
Shovel
Cookie sale sign

• *COSTUMES:*

Dawn's Red Riding Hood cape:

1. Maybe someone's parent can sew a cape, or
2. Maybe someone has a red hooded cape at home, or
3. Use a large piece of red cloth for the cape. Pin it around Dawn's neck. For the hood, use a red scarf. Tie it loosely around Dawn's head. Tuck the bottom under the top of the cape.

Jason's wolf suit:

1. Use a piece of fake fur. Cut out a hole in the center for his head (like a poncho). Wear brown or gray pants underneath and a dark shirt. If you don't have fake fur, you can use an old brown towel or bathmat.
2. Use a Halloween wolf mask, or make

one with mounting paper, cutting out eyes and painting the rest of the face.

3. Long, pointy fingernails can be made by wearing gloves. Make paper fingernails and glue them to the gloves.

Jim's costume:

1. A work shirt with overalls or dark-colored pants.
2. Jim might want to wear a bandanna around his neck.

• *MAKEUP:*

See *The Candy Corn Contest* for makeup for Ms. Rooney and the class.

For Jim: You might want to make Jim look like an older man:

1. Dust a little talcum powder on his hair.
2. Use a gray eyeliner to make his face look older. Ask him to smile into a mirror. Deepen his smile lines by marking them with the liner. Do the same for his frown lines.

• SCENE 1 •

DAWN *and* JASON *race into the classroom. They slam their books onto their desks.*

MS. R: Happy spring! Is everybody ready? It's idea time.
[DAWN *reaches into her pocket. She pulls out a piece of wrinkled paper. She smooths it out.*]
Who has an idea for us?
[DAWN, EMILY, BEAST, *and* TIMOTHY *put up their hands.*]
Yes, Beast.
[DAWN*'s hand stays up. She keeps waving it.*]

BEAST: We want to win the banner for the best class. Right?

MATTHEW: Right-a-reeno.

BEAST: My idea is . . .

[BEAST *takes a deep breath.*]

We could paint the hall.

EMILY: That would be *some* mess.

BEAST: It's a mess now. All brown and tan.

[*Everyone yells a different color for the hall to be painted.* MS. ROONEY *shakes her head.*]

MS. R: I don't think we'd be allowed to do that.

[DAWN *waves her hand harder.*]

Let's listen to Dawn's idea.

[DAWN *reads from her idea paper.*]

DAWN: Everyone knows I'm a great detective. Right?

[LINDA *makes a face.*]

JASON: You're the best.

ALEX: She's not bad.

[DAWN *reaches into her desk. She pulls out her polka dot detective hat. She slaps it on her head.*]

DAWN: We could find a mystery. I could solve it.

LINDA: No good.

[DAWN *makes a face.*]

DAWN: Why not?

LINDA: We don't have a mystery.
[MS. ROONEY *nods.*]

SEVERAL CHILDREN: That's right.

JILL: It's a good thing. I'm afraid of stuff like that.

MS. R: How about you, Timothy?
[DAWN *sits down. She rips up her idea paper.*]

TIMOTHY: Maybe we could put on a play.
[*Everyone nods and claps. The class goes to the stage. They start to practice.* DAWN *walks across the stage. She is wearing a red hooded cape. She is carrying a cake box in one hand, a can of chicken soup in the other, and a loaf of bread under*

her arm. She hears a swish, swish sound. She looks a little frightened and walks faster. From behind the curtain she sees hands with long, pointy fingernails and a hairy face.]

DAWN: I'm going to my grandmother's house.

[WOLF *springs from behind the curtain and grabs at* DAWN.]

WOLF: I'm going to *get* you!

[DAWN *screams.*]

DAWN: *Aaah!*

[MS. ROONEY *claps her hands.*]

MS. R: Wait a minute.

EMILY: That's all wrong. The wolf's not supposed to say that.

[DAWN *puts the cake box on the floor. She puts the bread and the soup on top of it. She puts her hands on her hips. She looks at the wolf.*]

DAWN: How come you tried to scare me, Jason?

[WOLF *disappears behind the curtain.*]

Jason?

MS. R: Jason?

[MS. ROONEY *stands up.* DAWN *goes to the back of the stage.*]

DAWN: Hey! He's not there!

[JASON *comes out from the other side of the stage. He wipes his mouth on his sleeve.*]

JASON: I had to get a drink.

DAWN: How did you get over there so fast?

SHERRI: You did the wolf part all wrong.

MATTHEW: You were supposed to growl.
[MATTHEW *makes a wolf face.*]
Grrr.

JASON: Wait a minute. I didn't even *do* the wolf part yet.
[JASON *crosses the stage on his hands and knees.*]
Yuff yiff. Ai ai ai. Hey . . . where's my wolf suit? Where are my fake fingernails?
[JASON *looks worried.*]
We've got to find them. My sister Peggy doesn't know I borrowed them. She's going to kill me.

MS. R: Look in the back. I'm sure you'll find them.

[MS. ROONEY *looks at her watch.*]

Oops. It's time to go home. We'd better line up.

[*The class lines up and exits the stage.* DAWN *and* JASON *stay behind.*]

DAWN: You weren't the wolf? Really?

JASON: Cross my toes. It was someone else. A person dressed in my sister Peggy's wolf suit.

[DAWN *looks as if she's ready to cry.*]

DAWN: A big person, I think. He said he was going to get me.

[DRAKE *and* LOUIE *enter the auditorium.*]

Oh! There's Drake Evans. He's the meanest boy in the school. I'm glad he's not in our class.

JASON: That's Louie, too. He's even bigger and meaner.

[DRAKE *and* LOUIE *see* DAWN *and* JASON.]

DRAKE: Arf, arf.

DAWN: You're not supposed to be here.

DRAKE: Dog voice.

LOUIE: Dog face.

JASON: *Grrr.*

[DAWN *sticks out her tongue.* DRAKE *and* LOUIE *leave the stage.*

They have mean looks on their faces.]
I just thought of something.

DAWN: What?

JASON: Maybe one of them was the wolf.

DAWN: You think Drake wore your wolf suit? Do you think Drake is going to get me?

JASON: I hope not. It's a mystery.
[DAWN *stands up tall.*]

DAWN: I'm the Polka Dot Private Eye. I'm the one who solves mysteries.

JASON: That's what I was thinking.

DAWN: I'll solve this mystery, too. I'll call it "The Secret at the Polk Street School."

End of Scene 1

• SCENE 2 •

DAWN *and* JASON *are at* DRAKE*'s house. They are hiding behind the bushes.* DRAKE *and* LOUIE *are sitting in front.*

DRAKE: We did it!

LOUIE: Yup.
[JASON *speaks in a loud whisper.*]

JASON: Did *what?*
[DAWN *pokes him and motions for him to be quiet.*]

DAWN: *Shhh!*

DRAKE: What was that noise?

LOUIE: The cat. A bird. Who cares?

DRAKE: Where did you put—

LOUIE: In the auditorium. In the stage closet.

[DAWN *and* JASON *look at each other.* DRAKE *leans over the bushes and sees* DAWN.]

DRAKE: Spies! Let's go, men!

[DRAKE *runs one way after* JASON. LOUIE *runs another way after* DAWN. DAWN *races for school. She goes into the auditorium. She heads for the closet.*]

DAWN: I wonder what Drake put in the closet? I bet it was the wolf suit.

[*She opens the closet door.*]

It's so dark in here.

[*She sings.*]

Don't be afraid. Be brave as a wave. Brave as a cave.

[*She puts her hand into the closet. She sings.*]

Plain air. Not a bear.

[DAWN *steps into the closet. We hear her speaking.*]

There should be a wolf suit somewhere. No. Just some old tools.

[*The closet door slams shut. The audience cannot see who has closed it. We hear* DAWN *banging.*]

Yeow! Somebody save me!

[*She hears footsteps.*]
Maybe it's Drake or Louie. Or someone else. Maybe they're going to get me!
[*The footsteps grow louder.* DAWN *begins to scream. The door bangs open.*]
I've got a gun!

JASON: Don't be silly. I thought you were brave.

DAWN: Of course I'm brave.
[DAWN *steps out of the closet.*]

JASON: Be very quiet. Jim is sweeping. We're not supposed to be in here.
[*Suddenly* JIM *walks in. He's holding a broom. He bangs it on the floor.*]

JIM: Dawn Bosco . . . Jason Bazyk. What are you doing?

DAWN: I was looking for something.

JIM: How about you?

JASON: I knew Dawn was looking for something. I thought she needed help.

DAWN: How did you know I was here?

JASON: I remembered what Louie said. I knew you'd go and look.

JIM: What will Ms. Rooney say?

JASON: Don't tell.

DAWN: Please.

JIM: You have to promise never to come to school this late again.

DAWN: We promise.

[JIM *exits the stage.*]

I'm hungry. It's almost dinnertime.

[*She reaches into her cape pocket.*]

Want some gum?

[DAWN *pulls out two sticks of gum. She finds a piece of paper.*]

JASON: What's that paper?

[DAWN *opens the paper and reads.*]

DAWN: Listen! DAWN BOSCO, I'M GOING TO GET YOU. JASON, TOO.

JASON: Who's it from?

DAWN: It's signed: THE WOLF.

JASON: Let me see that.

[JASON *takes the paper.*]

It smells funny.

[DAWN *holds it up to her nose.*]

DAWN: It *does* smell strange. It smells like something burnt.

[DAWN *raises her shoulders in the air.* DAWN *and* JASON *exit the stage.*]

End of Scene 2

• SCENE 3 •

The next day everyone enters the classroom. Several other children march across the front of the stage.

EMILY: Hey! There goes Mrs. Gates's class.

TIMOTHY: Drake is carrying a shovel. [DAWN *taps* JASON.]

DAWN: There was a shovel in the closet last night.

JASON: Louie said he put something in the closet.

DAWN: Just an old shovel? He wasn't talking about the wolf suit?

JASON: Then Drake isn't the wolf.

MS. R: Isn't it lovely? Mrs. Gates's class is planting a flower garden for the school. They want to win the banner, too.

DAWN: Hey! What's this?
[DAWN *holds up her can of soup and the bread.*]

EMILY: Someone took a big bite out of the bread.

SHERRI: It was probably Beast. He likes to fool around.

DAWN: There are pointy teeth marks in it. Huge ones.

TIMOTHY: Maybe a dog.

DAWN: Maybe a wolf.

MS. R: It's recess time. Ms. Smith's class is having a bake sale. You may go, if you want.

[*On the auditorium side of the stage, children are setting up a table with cookies. A huge sign in front of the table reads:* HELP US WIN THE BANNER. BUY A COOKIE FOR THE SCHOOL. DAWN *and* JASON *leave the classroom to buy some.*]

JASON: Don't get chocolate. My sister Peggy made them. She burned them a little.

PEGGY: Bunny brain. Be quiet.

DAWN: I'll take an oatmeal cookie.

PEGGY: Here you are, Red Riding Hood.

[DAWN *and* JASON *walk back to the classroom.* DAWN *stops suddenly inside the door.*]

DAWN: Listen! I *know* who the wolf is.

JASON: Tell me.

EMILY: Tell me, too.

DAWN: It's Peggy.

EVERYONE: Peggy? Jason's sister? I don't believe it.

DAWN: Peggy called me Red Riding Hood.

LINDA: So?

DAWN: The play was a surprise. How did she know I was Red Riding Hood?

EMILY: That's right. How did she know?

JASON: She's always sneaking around. She must have seen us practicing.

LINDA: She was probably angry that you borrowed her wolf suit.

DAWN: She put the wolf note in my Red Riding Hood cape.

JASON: A scary one.

DAWN: One that smelled like burnt cookies.

EMILY: Peggy made teeth marks in the bread, too.

DAWN: Peggy wanted to scare us. She didn't want us to win the banner. But I, Dawn, the Polka Dot Private Eye, once again solved the mystery!
[*She bows slightly, trying to look modest.*]

MS. R: Time for the play. Is everybody ready?
[*They put on their costumes. The class marches to the stage side. They sit in a circle around the*

stage. JASON *hides behind someone.* DAWN *stands in the middle.*]

EMILY: This is going to be good.

BEAST: It's going to be great.

TIMOTHY: Better than a flower garden.

LINDA: Better than a cookie sale.
[DAWN *speaks to the audience in a loud voice.*]

DAWN: I'm going to my grandmother's house.

[*Curtain*]

Trying Out . . . Different Ideas

"Whew," says Ms. Rooney. "I *told* you mysteries are hard."

"Let's try something easy next," says Beast.

"That's for me," says Matthew.

"How about something for my little sister Stacy?" says Emily.

Ms. Rooney looks up at the ceiling. "We could do *Fancy Feet*. It's short, it's easy. And there's something else, too."

"I hope it's food," says Matthew.

Ms. Rooney shakes her head. "No. It's that this play is easy to change around."

Emily frowns. "It's about a classroom store and a girl who wants to buy gold shoes."

"That's right," Ms. Rooney says. "But if you don't have gold shoes, you can use anything else."

"The girl may want to buy a game or a purse or a hat—" says Sherri.

"It wouldn't have to be a girl, either," says Timothy. "It could be a boy who wanted something—"

"Like a pizza," says Beast.

"Well, maybe not a pizza," says Ms. Rooney. "But you've got the idea. Read the play first. Then take a pencil. See if you can come up with some other ideas. The main thing to remember is that the main person in the story grows up a little by the end of the play."

Acting . . .
FANCY FEET

• *CHARACTERS (The people in the play):*

MRS. ZACHARY

The class: A.J., BILLY, EDDIE, FRANK, JIWON, LISA, MARIA, MIKE, PATTY, STACY, TWANA

Other: EMILY

• *SETTING (What the stage looks like):*

Mrs. Zachary's classroom, with a desk for Mrs. Zachary and desks for the children. There are also a few plants. On one side of the classroom is the store. You will need a bookcase with a table in front.

• *PROPERTIES (Things you'll need):*

Band-Aids
Gold paper with a shiny *S*
Play money
Watering can
Brown paper bag

Wastebasket
Bunny
Bank
Green yo-yo
Horse-on-a-stick
Gold high-heel shoes, toy bear, books, games, and other items that could be sold in a school store
Toy chest filled with junky old toys

• *COSTUMES:*

Mrs. Zachary might wear slacks and a loose top. She might wear her hair up on top of her head. Maybe she has a pencil stuck behind one ear.

Children in Mrs. Zachary's class will wear everyday school clothes. Hint: Bright colors show up best onstage.

Stacy will wear a school dress or a skirt, so the audience can see the cut on her knee, and sneakers.

Eddie will wear a pair of jeans with a hole in the knee. (If you don't have jeans with holes, you can always draw a picture of a hole and tape it to the knee of a pair of jeans.)

- *MAKEUP:*

Mrs. Zachary would certainly wear lipstick, blush, and eye makeup. For the children, see makeup suggestions for *The Candy Corn Contest*.

• SCENE 1 •

STACY *and* EDDIE *enter* MRS. ZACHARY*'s room.* STACY *is limping. They walk toward* MRS. ZACHARY*'s desk.*

STACY: I hope your mom won't be mad about the hole in your jeans. I didn't mean to bump into you.

EDDIE: That's all right. Mrs. Zachary says the Band-Aids are on her desk. Is your knee still bleeding?

STACY: I don't think so.
[STACY *and* EDDIE *look on* MRS. ZACHARY*'s desk.*]

EDDIE: Great stuff here.

[STACY *picks up a piece of gold paper with a shiny* S.]

STACY: I'll bet it's going to be *S* week. [STACY *puts down the piece of paper. She picks up two Band-Aids. She pulls one open.* EDDIE *sits on the floor. He looks at his jeans.*]

EDDIE: I could put a Band-Aid on my jeans. You wouldn't even see the hole.

STACY: I need them for my knee.

EDDIE: You don't need both. That cut is smaller than an ant. A little tiny ant.

STACY: It is *not*.

[STACY *slaps one Band-Aid on her knee straight up and down. She puts the other one on sideways.* EDDIE *looks angry.*]

EDDIE: Let's go.

STACY: I wonder what's in Mrs. Zachary's drawer?

EDDIE: My mother says don't open anyone's dresser drawers.

STACY: Does this look like a dresser? This is a desk.
[STACY *starts to open the drawer.*]

EDDIE: Let's get out of here. I don't want to be in trouble.

STACY: Look . . . a *million* dollars!

EDDIE: Wow!

STACY: Mrs. Zachary is rich.
[*They hear the class coming.* STACY *slams the drawer shut. The class enters. Everyone takes a seat.*]

MRS. Z: We start a new letter today. Who can guess?
[STACY *waves her hand high. She*

makes S *sounds. Other children have their hands raised, too.* EDDIE *is not paying attention.*]

MRS. Z: You may guess, Eddie.

EDDIE: Five.

MRS. Z: That's a number. We're doing letters.
[STACY *laughs a little.* PATTY *calls out.*]

PATTY: Is it *X*?

MRS. Z: *X* is a nice letter. But that's not the one.
[STACY *kneels up on her chair.*]

STACY: *SSSSS.*

MRS. Z: Stacy, please sit down.

[STACY *slides down.* EDDIE *stands up.*]

EDDIE: It's *S.*

STACY: No fair.

MRS. Z: Right, Edward. What a good guess.

[STACY *puts her fingers in her mouth. She pulls her lips open wide. She sticks her tongue out at* EDDIE.]

STACY: I don't think Eddie was guessing.

[MRS. ZACHARY *doesn't hear. She holds up the gold paper with the shiny* S.]

MRS. Z: Do you know why this letter is special?

[STACY *waves her hand around.*]

STACY: It says my name.

MRS. Z: Yes, indeed. *SSSS* . . . Stacy. Let's all make the *S* sound.
[*The class says* SSSS.]
Wonderful. Here comes a surprise.
[MRS. ZACHARY *opens her desk*

drawer. She takes out a pile of dollar bills.]

A.J.: Wow!

STACY: Mrs. Zachary is rich. I knew it. [STACY *covers her mouth.]*

MRS. Z: We're going to have a store.

JIWON: *S* for store.

MRS. Z: Yes, indeed.

STACY: Yes, indeed.

MRS. Z: It will be right here in the classroom. When you go home today, look around. Find something you'd like to sell at the store. With the money you earn, you can buy things.

MARIA: Is it real money?

MRS. Z: No, it's just-for-fun money.

A.J.: How do we earn it?

MRS. Z: You can earn money by doing your work. Or you can earn it by good behavior.
[STACY *turns to* EDDIE.]

STACY: I'm going to be so good, I'll buy out the store.

End of Scene 1

• SCENE 2 •

The curtain is closed. On the side of the stage is a toy chest filled with STACY*'s old toys.* STACY *kneels in front of it. She is singing.*

STACY: Look, look, looking. What's no, no good?
[*She holds up a green yo-yo. The string is missing. Her sister* EMILY *comes toward her.*]

EMILY: What a piece of junk.

STACY: It's for the class store, store, store.
[STACY *replies, still singing.*]

EMILY: We had one in Mrs. Zachary's class, too.
[EMILY *puts her hands on her hips.*]
You can't bring that. It's awful.
[STACY *digs deeper into the box. She holds up a horse-on-a-stick.*]

STACY: How about this?

EMILY: Terrible. Bring something nice.
[EMILY *looks around.*]
How about that bank?

STACY: My bunny bank? My favorite old bunny bank?

EMILY: Yes.

STACY: I *love* that bank. I got it for my birthday. Besides, it has fifty cents in it. I can't get it out. [STACY'*s head disappears into the chest. She holds up a book.*]

EMILY: That scribble scrabble book?

STACY: Too bad. I'm not bringing my good stuff.

End of Scene 2

• SCENE 3 •

It's the next day. MRS. ZACHARY *is working on the store.* JIWON *and* PATTY *are helping.* STACY *and* EDDIE *are watering the plants. They watch.* MRS. ZACHARY *puts a bear on the top shelf.*

EDDIE: That's my bear.

STACY: Not such a hot bear.

EDDIE: I gave it a karate chop.

STACY: I brought a book.

MRS. Z: Does anyone else have something for the store?
[JIWON *walks to* MRS. ZACHARY. *She is holding a brown paper bag.*]

JIWON: Look what *I* brought.

[JIWON *reaches into the bag. She takes out a pair of shoes. They are gold shoes for a woman.*]

I wanted to bring something really nice to share.

STACY: Me, too.

TWANA: Do you think that scribbly book is nice?

[STACY *looks sad.* JIWON *puts on the shoes. She dances around in front of the class.* STACY *taps* EDDIE *on the shoulder.*]

STACY: Those are the most beautiful shoes I ever saw. If they were mine, I'd never give them away.

[STACY *starts dancing, too. She spills water on the floor.*]

FRANK: You made a big mess.

[STACY *makes a witch face at him.*]

Mrs. Zachary, Stacy made a mess. She made a witch face, too.

[MRS. ZACHARY *shakes her head at* STACY. STACY *looks really sad. She turns to* EDDIE.]

STACY: I'll never earn any just-for-fun money. I'll never get those shoes.

End of Scene 3

• SCENE 4 •

STACY *enters the classroom alone. She goes over to the store. She takes the gold shoes off the shelf and puts them on.*

STACY: Perfect.

[STACY *walks around. The heels are high.* STACY *has trouble walking.*]

I don't care if Mrs. Zachary made me stay inside for recess. I'm not sorry I hit Twana. She was mean to me. I'd rather

play with these shoes, anyway.

[*She dances in the shoes and sings.*]

La dee, la dee, dee.

[*She hears the class coming. She takes off the shoes. She is too far from the shelf to put them back. Scared, she throws them in the wastebasket.*]

I'll get them out later.

[STACY *grabs her sneakers. She runs to her seat. She slides into the sneakers.*]

I hope Mrs. Zachary doesn't see the shoes in the basket. I'm in enough trouble. I'm glad it's time to go home.

End of Scene 4

• SCENE 5 •

The class enters the room. STACY *goes over to the wastebasket. She speaks to herself.*

STACY: Oh, *no!* The shoes are gone! Jim, the custodian, must have emptied the basket.
[STACY *goes to the store. She looks for the shoes on the shelf.*]
They're not on the shelf, either.
[JIWON *looks at the store. She goes closer. She stands there a moment. Then she goes to* MRS. ZACHARY'S *desk.*]

JIWON: My shoes are gone.

MRS. Z: We didn't sell them, did we?
[JIWON *shakes her head.*]

PATTY: I wanted those shoes. I had almost enough just-for-fun money.

LISA: Me, too.

MRS. Z: Oh, dear. What could have happened to them?

STACY: Maybe someone threw them out by accident.

LISA: I don't think so.

MIKE: I don't think so, either.

BILLY: I think someone took them.

STACY: It wasn't me.

A.J.: It wasn't me, either. I don't wear high heels.
[*He and* EDDIE *laugh.*]

JIWON: What are we going to do?

MRS. Z: Don't worry. We'll find them. Let's all look hard.

[*Everyone runs around looking for the shoes.* STACY *makes believe she's looking, too.* TWANA *taps* STACY *on the shoulder.*]

TWANA: Stealing Stacy.

A.J.: Stacy's a nice girl. She wouldn't steal anything.

MRS. Z: I'm sorry. We have to stop looking now. It's time for lunch.

[*The class lines up and leaves the room.* STACY *stays behind. She walks up to* MRS. ZACHARY.]

STACY: I have something to tell you . . .

End of Scene 5

• SCENE 6 •

Next day. The class enters the room. STACY *is carrying a paper bag. She brings it to* MRS. ZACHARY*'s desk.*

MRS. Z: What's this?

STACY: It's a bank. My best birthday bank. It's for the store. It has fifty cents inside for new shoes.

[*Curtain*]